I AM READING

Tooth Fairy in Trouble

JULIA JARMAN

ILLUSTRATED BY

MIRIAM LATIMER

KINGFISHER
NEW YORK

To Maya, a magical girl—J. J.
To Seb, love from Mimi

Text copyright © 2008 by Julia Jarman
Illustrations copyright © 2008 by Miriam Latimer
KINGFISHER
Published in the United States by Kingfisher, an imprint of Henry Holt and Company LLC,
175 Fifth Avenue, New York, New York 10010. First published in Great Britain by Kingfisher
Publications plc, a imprint of Macmillan Children's Books, London.

Distributed in Canada by H. B. Fenn and Company Ltd.

Library of Congress Cataloging-in-Publication Data
has been applied for.

ISBN: 978-0-7534-6236-2

Kingfisher books are available for special promotions and premiums.
For details contact: Director of Special Markets, Holtzbrinck Publishers.

First American Edition August 2008
Printed in China
1 3 5 7 9 8 6 4 2
1TR/1207/WKT/SC(SC)/IISMA/C

Contents

Chapter One

Tooth Fairy was in trouble.

It was getting light, but she still hadn't finished her tooth-collecting route on The Surface.

She had to get back to Fairyland soon.

"Oh no!" she said to herself as she flew into the next bedroom on her route. The boy in bed was waking up.

Tooth Fairy froze. The boy felt underneath his pillow—and found his teeth. There were two of them, yucky and yellowy brown.

"MOM!" The boy cried
for his mother and threw
the teeth onto the floor.
"Tooth Fairy hasn't COME!"

Tooth Fairy flew
down, found one
tooth, and put it
into her sack.

6

Then his mother appeared.

"See! No money!" said the boy as
he pointed at his bed.
"But, Norman, your teeth aren't here,"
said his mother.

"Look on the floor, silly!"
said Norman.

Tooth Fairy wanted to fix this horrible

boy with a spell.

But she could feel herself

becoming visible.

Her magic powers were

draining away.

That is what happens when fairies

stay on The Surface for too long.

She dived underneath the bed.
"What was that?" Nasty Norman
moved surprisingly quickly.
Has he seen me? thought Tooth Fairy
as he peered underneath the bed.
Tooth Fairy stayed as far back
as she could.

She could see his gap-toothed mouth
and piercing eyes. Tooth Fairy was sure
that the boy could see her. There was
a nasty smile on his face.

Suddenly his hand shot forward.

But Tooth Fairy was faster.

Whoosh!

She shot past his hand . . .

. . . up to the window
and then out of it.

Chapter Two

"Phew!" said Tooth Fairy, but she saw

that the street was busy.

Could she reach the door to Fairyland

without being seen?

The entrance to Fairyland was a little
door at the foot of an old oak tree in
Woodland Park. *Whoosh!*
'Made it!" said Tooth Fairy.
But a huge dog was lifting its hind leg.

"Open the door!
Zaraband!
Whiz me back
to Fairyland!"
She waved her
wand frantically . . .

The dog moved
and the door
opened!
Whiz!
She hurried
to Fairyland.

"How wonderful to be back!" said Tooth Fairy, feeling very relieved.

Some Flower Fairies were there.
"Foxglove! Bluebell! Primrose!
I've had a terrible night."

But Bluebell shouted, "Stay there,
Tooth Fairy! We don't want any more
stinky teeth."

"They're not stinky," said Tooth Fairy.

Most of them were white and shiny.

"That one is." Bluebell pointed at

Nasty Norman's yucky brown tooth.

It was peeping out of Tooth Fairy's sack.

"There are too many teeth in Fairyland,"
said Primrose more kindly.
"Look at the Tooth Dump.
It's so big. What if it collapsed
and squashed us?"

"Tooth Dump? That's the Royal Tooth Collection," said Tooth Fairy. But she had to admit that it did look dangerous.

"I'll think about it," she replied.
"But what can I do? I'm the Tooth
Fairy," she said to herself.

Collecting teeth and putting money
under children's pillows was her job.
If she didn't do it, they would be sad.

The journey to her house was miserable.

She heard the fairies sing a horrible song:

"Fly away as fast as you can.

Tooth Fairy smells

like a garbage man!"

When they saw her coming, they flew

away. It made Tooth Fairy sad.

And as if that wasn't enough for poor Tooth Fairy, back on The Surface Nasty Norman was setting a trap for her. He was sticking a tooth to the floor with glue, and he had gotten ahold of a butterfly net.

Chapter Three

When she got home, Tooth Fairy went straight to bed.

But she was woken up by a Royal Goblin ringing a bell.

"The Fairy Queen wants to see you, NOW!"

"Why?" Tooth Fairy said with a yawn.

"She'll tell you herself," he said.

The Fairy Queen looked very angry.

"Tooth Fairy, I have had a lot of complaints.

You are forgetting to collect teeth.

You are forgetting to leave money.

Last night you missed a whole street.

What do you have to say for yourself?"

Tooth Fairy took a deep breath.

"It's so *hard*, your majesty.

There's not enough time.

Surface children go to bed so late, and

some of them are horrible, and . . ."

The Queen was tapping her wand

impatiently.

"Tooth Fairy, you must start earlier.

You are *invisible* on The Surface."

But not if I stay there too long,

Tooth Fairy thought.

But she didn't say that.

She didn't dare.

Chapter Four

That night, Tooth Fairy set off early.
But when she reached the door to
The Surface, the Flower Fairies were
waiting for her. Dandelion said,
"DON'T bring any teeth back, okay?"

Tooth Fairy said boldly, "The Fairy
Queen told me that I have to. So there."
But she felt very worried, mostly about
the Tooth Dump.
It did look dangerous.

At first, all went well.

In a few minutes, her sack was full—

with nice, clean teeth.

Most of the children were great.

They brushed their teeth.

They didn't eat too much candy.

One boy had even written her

a thank-you letter!

It was Joe and his sister, Sylvie, who
gave her a very good idea.

They had built a whole town out
of blocks—houses, sidewalks,
patios, furniture.

What if fairies built things from teeth?

Tooth Fairy thought.

We could have a Royal Tooth Recycling

Factory!

Longing to get back and tell everyone

her good idea, Tooth Fairy did her

route very fast . . .

. . . until she came to Nasty Norman's.
She'd left him until last.

Chapter Five

At first, Tooth Fairy hovered outside.
Norman's tooth was still on the floor.
Should I leave it there? she wondered.
No. The Fairy Queen will be angry.

Whoosh!

She flew in.

Thwack!

A net trapped her.

Norman was staring at her.

"Gotcha, Tooth Fairy!"

Tooth Fairy was in big trouble.

She could feel herself becoming visible.

Her fairy powers were draining away.

Hoping that she still had some powers

left, she whirled her wand.

'Izzy wizzy

If you don't let me out!

Or see your nose

Turn into a snout."

The silly boy laughed—

and didn't see his nose start to flatten!

'Izzy wizzy

Let me out of here!

Or see yourself

With floppy pig's ears."

He didn't see his

ears start to change.

"Izzy wizzy

Let me out of this jail!

Or see your bottom

Get a curly tail!"

The silly boy

didn't see his

bottom getting

big and fat.

He didn't see a

curly tail peep out

of his pajamas.

But his mother did!
"Honey, what's the
matter?"
"Oink!"
Norman's mother
screamed. Norman
dropped the net,
and Tooth Fairy
made her escape!

She was soon back in Fairyland.
The fairies thought that her Royal
Tooth Recycling Factory was terrific!
Building things was fun, and
they made many useful creations.

They made a swimming pool,
a summer house, and a new
palace for the Fairy Queen.

"Thank you, Tooth Fairy. You're great!'
said the Fairy Queen.

"It's a pleasure," replied Tooth Fairy
with a big smile on her face.

About the author and illustrator

Julia Jarman used to be a teacher, and she still spends a lot of time at schools talking to children. She loves writing stories and has published more than 100 books for children. Julia says, "I think some fairies are silly, but Tooth Fairy is great. She's kind and helpful and brave, and I wanted to write a story about her."

Miriam Latimer loves illustrating children's books and has had many picture books published. She always carries her sketchbook with her, and she loves daydreaming and imagining new characters to draw. Miriam says, "I love the idea of thinking up new ways to recycle, just like Tooth Fairy."

Strategies for Independent Readers

Predict

Think about the cover, illustrations, and the title
of the book. What do you think this book will be about
While you are reading think about what may
happen next and why.

Monitor

As you read ask yourself if what you're reading makes sense.
If it doesn't, reread, look at the illustrations, or read ahead.

Question

Ask yourself questions about important ideas
in the story such as what the characters might
do or what you might learn.

Phonics

If there is a word that you do not know, look carefully
at the letters, sounds, and word parts that you do know.
Blend the sounds to read the word. Ask yourself if this is
a word you know. Does it make sense in the sentence?

Summarize

Think about the characters, the setting where the
story takes place, and the problem the characters faced
in the story. Tell the important ideas in the beginning,
middle, and end of the story.

Evaluate

Ask yourself questions like: Did you like the story?
Why or why not? How did the author make the story
come alive? How did the author make the story fun to
read? How well did you understand the story? Maybe
you can understand it better if you read it again!